For Max, with love — AM
For Bruno, with love — JJ

BLOOMSBURY
CHILDREN'S
BOOKS

Published by Bloomsbury, New York and London
Distributed to the trade by Holtzbrinck Publishers

Library of Congress Cataloging-in-Publication Data:
McAllister, Angela.
Harry's Box / by Angela McAllister; illustrated by Jenny Jones.--1st U.S. ed. p. cm.
Summary: A young boy and his dog spend an afternoon playing with a cardboard box
and imagining that it has become all sorts of exciting things.
ISBN 1-58234-772-7 (alk. paper)
[1. Boxes--Fiction. 2. Imagination--Fiction. 3. Play--Fiction. 4. Dogs--Fiction]
I. Jones, Jenny, ill. II. Title.
PZ7.M11714 Har 2003   [E]dc-21   2002027822

Printed in Hong Kong by South China Printing Co.
First U.S. Edition 2003
1 3 5 7 9 10 8 6 4 2

Bloomsbury USA Children's Books
175 Fifth Avenue
New York, New York 10010

Harry's Box

By Angela McAllister

Illustrated by Jenny Jones

BLOOMSBURY
CHILDREN'S
BOOKS

Harry helped his mother at the supermarket.
He put all the shopping in the box and,

when they got home, he took
all the shopping out of the box.

So his mother gave Harry the box to play in.
First he put it in the kitchen.

There it became a shop
full of toys, treats and treasures.

But a difficult customer wanted
bones and old slippers.

"I can't please everybody,"
said Harry the Shopkeeper.

Then he put the box in the garden.

There it became a dangerous lion's den where a roaring lion and a growling bear waited to frighten somebody.

But only a brave dog passed by
and barked at the wild animals.

"Lions just aren't scary enough,"
sighed Harry the Lion.

So then he put the box in the bathroom.

And there it became a pirate ship
sailing on the stormy seas in search of treasure.

A shipwrecked sailor said there was
something precious buried in the sand.

"I expect it will be a bone," said Harry the Pirate.

Next he put the box under the table.

There it became a sandy cave
on the seabed where an octopus waved
his eight arms to catch fish for supper.

But only a dog-fish swam by and
he was much too hairy to eat.

"I hope that there are fish fingers for dinner," said Harry the Octopus.

Then he put the box in his bedroom.

There it became a castle
on a high hill where a king and
his soldiers were ready for battle.

But when the foe arrived she brought
the king's favorite cookies.

"Let's be friends!" said Harry the King.

So then he put the box behind the sofa.

And there it became a warm, snug bed where Harry and Wolfie dreamt about

dog food

and lions

and pirates

and octopuses

and castles

and all the boxes they could make tomorrow...

ЦJ